Owl and 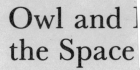 the Space

It's Billy's half term and he has a whole week's holiday. Each day, Billy's 'Spaceman' friend receives a special message telling him which Space Day it is – and what special event the day holds in store . . .

Owl and Billy and the Space Days

MARTIN WADDELL

Illustrated by Carolyn Dinan

A Magnet Book

Dedication
A book for the small ones
at St Mary's Boys Primary
School, Newcastle

First published in Great Britain 1988
by Methuen Children's Books Ltd
This edition first published 1989
by Magnet Paperbacks
Michelin House, 81 Fulham Road, London SW3 6RB
Text copyright © 1988 Martin Waddell
Illustrations copyright © 1988 Carolyn Dinan
Printed in Great Britain
by Cox & Wyman Ltd, Reading

ISBN 0 416 13932 9

Contents

1 *Moonday*

It was Monday morning, but Billy Ogle
didn't have to go to school because he had a
whole week's half-term break. He stayed in
the garden playing with his special friends,
Owl and Woggly Man.

They played Watching Ants and Race-
track (Billy won because Billy had the tricycle) and Flying (Woggly Man won because
he flew highest when Billy threw him) and
Kick-the-Bins.

'Billy!' Mum said. 'Stop that!'

'Why?' said Billy.

'Because it makes a dreadful noise!' said
Mum.

'Can we have Bin Band instead?' asked

7

Billy.

'No,' said Mum.

'Owl wants to have a Bin Band,' Billy said.

'Tell Owl it's absolutely forbidden!' said Mum.

So Billy told Owl, and Owl said they should go to Mr Bennet's and have a Bin Band there instead, because Mr Bennet invented Bin Bands. Mr Bennet was always

inventing things. He was a Spaceman who lived in the Old Folks, but nobody knew he was a Spaceman except Owl and Billy and Woggly Man and Mum. It was a secret.

They went to Mr Bennet's.

'Hullo, Mr Bennet,' said Billy. 'Owl wants to have a Bin Band at your house, because Mum won't let us at ours.'

'I don't know that I feel up to Bin Bands this morning, Billy,' said Mr Bennet.

'Why not?' said Billy.

Mr Bennet thought for a bit, and then he said. 'Because it's *Moon*day.'

Billy told Owl, and Owl said it wasn't Moonday, it was Monday, so Billy told Mr Bennet.

'It's Monday, the first day of my holiday!' said Billy. 'Saturday and Sunday don't count, because they aren't school days.'

'And *Moon*day is *my* holiday, Billy!' said Mr Bennet.

'Because you're a Spaceman?' asked Billy.

And Mr Bennett went which means 'YES' in Secret Sign Language.

Billy went which means 'I'LL
HAVE TO THINK ABOUT IT'.

And he sat and thought about it.
'You're on holiday and we're on holiday,'
Billy said.

 went Mr Bennet.
'Owl says if we're all on holiday, we can
have a Bin Band together!' said Billy.

 went Mr Bennet.

 is the Secret Sign for 'NO',
and Owl thought that Mr Bennet had got
mixed up.

'Owl thinks you meant to go '
said Billy, doing it.

'Owl's wrong,' said Mr Bennet. 'Spacemen don't have Bin Bands on Moondays.
On Moondays Spacemen moon-about. That
means they keep very quiet and do nothing,
and see nothing, and think nothing and

smoke their pipes.'

'Oh,' said Billy, sounding very disappointed. 'Don't they play with their friends?'

'It depends on how much mooning they can get in early in the day.' said Mr Bennet. 'If they get mooning right up to tea-time, without any interruption at all, *then* they play with their friends.'

'What do they play?' said Billy.

'Moon Games!' said Mr Bennet.

'Owl wants to know what Moon Games *are*,' Billy said.

'Tell Owl to wait and see,' said Mr Bennet, and then he sat down in his chair and filled his pipe and lit it and puffed and closed his eyes.

'Are you mooning?' Billy asked.

'Not properly,' said Mr Bennet.

'Why not?'

'Because people keep asking me questions!' said Mr Bennet.

Billy told Owl, and Owl said he thought they ought to go home and come back after tea for the Moon Games, so they did.

'Mr Bennet's mooning,' Billy told Mum.

'Oh dear,' said Mum. 'Is he all right?'

'Yes,' said Billy. 'He's keeping quiet and doing nothing and seeing nothing and thinking nothing and smoking his pipe until after tea-time, and then he's playing Moon Games with us.'

'That's very good of him,' said Mum.

'Owl kept asking him questions, and he couldn't moon properly,' said Billy.

'Silly Owl!' said Mum.

'Owl doesn't know what Moon Games are,' said Billy. 'Owl thinks you should go and ask Mr Bennet what Moon Games are, so we'll know if we want to play them. But I told Owl you wouldn't, because that would mean Mr Bennet wouldn't get mooning right up to tea-time!'

'Quite right, Billy,' said Mum, and instead of asking Mr Bennet questions she took Owl and Billy to the swings after lunch, but Woggly Man didn't come because he wanted to moon. He stayed at home in the playbox.

Then they went to the shops and the library and then Mum's hat blew away and Billy got it and then they went home and

Mum and Billy and Owl sat down and mooned.

'Owl's fed up with mooning, Mum,' Billy said. 'He wants to have a Bin Band.'

'A Moonday one?' said Mum.
'What's a Moonday one?' asked Billy.

'One that doesn't make any sound, so it doesn't interrupt all the people who are mooning,' said Mum.

Billy told Owl, but Owl said there was nobody to interrupt, so Billy told Mum.

'Yes there is!' said Mum. 'There's me and Mr Bennet and Woggly Man. We're all mooning up until tea-time, which is why you can only have a Moonday Bin Band.'

So Owl and Billy had a Moonday Bin Band that made hardly any noise at all and then they had a Moonday Tip Toe competition up and down the stairs and then the doorbell went BRIIING-BRIING-BRIING!

Mum stopped mooning, and went to the door.

'Hullo, Mr Bennet,' she said.

'I've come for Owl and Billy,' Mr Bennet said.

'I thought that was *after* tea-time,' Mum said.

'They've been so good letting me moon that I'm inviting them for Moonday tea!' said Mr Bennet. 'You can come too!'

So Mum and Owl and Billy and Woggly

Man all went round to Mr Bennet's for Moonday tea.

They had Moon-biscuits and Moon-burgers and Moon-wine (which was very like orange juice) and then they had Moon Games.

Billy won the Moon Shoot, because he knocked the most Moon-sweets off the chair with the Moon Marble.

Owl won the Moon Hide because no-one could find him when he hid down the sofa.

'I knew where he was, but I didn't tell anybody because I wanted him to win,' Billy said, and Owl let Billy have his Moon-sweet Prize, because Owls don't like sweets.

'It's Moon Treasure time!' said Mr Bennet.

'Oooh!' said Billy. 'What is the Moon Treasure?'

'You'll find out when you find it!' said Mr Bennet. 'First you have to follow the stars.'

'What stars?' said Mum.

But Billy knew what stars, because he'd noticed them when he first came in. They were little yellow stars, grouped together like this,

to make an arrow.

The first arrow pointed out into the hall, and in the hall there was another one, like this,

pointing into the kitchen.

And in the kitchen there was another one like this,

pointing into the cupboard.

And in the cupboard there was a big circle of stars, with the Moon Treasure Box in the middle, like this:

'Shall I open it?' asked Billy, and Mr Bennet said yes. Billy opened the Treasure Box, and it was all filled up with chocolates, wrapped in shiny gold paper, like Moon Pirate doubloons!

Billy ate lots and lots, some for himself, and some for Owl, because Owls get messy with chocolates, and there were still plenty left over to take home for supper time.

'Time to go home now, Billy,' said Mum. 'Say thank you very much to Mr Bennet.'

'Thank you very much, Mr Bennet,' said Billy.

Then Owl whispered something to Billy, and Billy told Mr Bennet.

'Owl says thank you very much too, and can we come and have another Moonday tomorrow?'

Mr Bennet went which means NO.

'Why not?' said Billy.

'Because today is Moonday,' said Mr Bennet. 'Tomorrow is quite a different day.'

'*What* day is it?' demanded Billy.

'Come round to my house tomorrow at two o'clock, and you'll find out!' said Mr Bennet.

'Why two o'clock?' said Billy.

'Wait and see!' said Mr Bennet.

2 Chooseday

'Mum,' said Billy. 'Owl wants to know what day it is.'

'Tuesday,' said Mum.

'Not what day it is *here*,' said Billy. 'What day it is at Mr Bennet's.'

'Haven't a clue,' said Mum. 'I can't keep up with these Space Days of Mr Bennet's.'

'Do you think that is what they are?' Billy asked.

'Must be,' said Mum. 'He's a Spaceman, isn't he?'

Owl and Billy and Woggly Man went to Mr Bennet's house, and Billy rang the bell.

'Hullo, Billy,' said Mr Bennet, opening the door.

'It's two o'clock!' Billy said.

'How do you know?' said Mr Bennet. 'You haven't got a watch.'

'I know because I'm *here*,' said Billy. 'You said I had to come at two o'clock and you said it was a special day and you said I would find out what day it was if I came at two.'

'Right!' said Mr Bennet.

'What day is it then?' demanded Billy.

'Twoes-day!' said Mr Bennet. 'On Twoes-day, there is two of everything!' And he took Owl and Billy and Woggly Man inside his house.

'Sit down,' he said, and they sat down.

'Not that way!' said Mr Bennet. 'On Twoesday you have to sit down on two chairs, both at the same time!' and he showed them how to do it.

'Is that all?' Billy said.

'No,' said Mr Bennet. And he showed them how to drink two drinks, both at the same time, with two glasses and two straws. One was lemon and one was orange, and they tasted funny. Then he smoked two pipes, both puffing at the same time, and

making Space smoke rings.

'You try two sweets,' said Mr Bennet.

'I might choke,' said Billy.

'Right!' said Mr Bennet. 'Two sweets, one after the other will do.'

So Billy had two green sweets, and Owl had two yellow sweets, and Woggly Man had two red sweets. Woggly Man and Owl didn't finished theirs, so Billy had to help them.

'Thank you very much for our sweets, Mr

Bennet,' Billy said.

Mr Bennet said that that was all right.

He was only smoking *one* of his two pipes, because he said he hadn't enough puff to keep the two going at once, even though it was Twoesday, so he smoked them one at a time, changing pipes between puffs.

Owl and Billy and Woggly Man sat there watching him do it.

Owl got fed up.

He told Billy about it, and Billy told Mr Bennet.

'Owl doesn't like Twoesday, Mr Bennet,' he said.

'Oh dear!' said Mr Bennet. 'Why not?'

'Because we've got nothing to do,' said Billy. 'Usually when we come to your house there's something to do, but on Twoesday there isn't.'

'I think I'd better check that it *is* Twoesday,' said Mr Bennet. 'Perhaps I got the Space Message wrong.'

They waited and waited and waited for another Space Message to come, while Mr Bennet puffed his pipe.

Then Mr Bennet said, 'The message is

23

coming. The message says: IT'S CHOOSE-DAY, NOT TWOESDAY!'

'Chooseday?' said Billy. 'What's that?'

'It means *you* choose day,' said Mr Bennet. 'You choose what you want to do.'

Owl and Billy and Woggly Man thought about it. Owl wanted to go to the park and Woggly Man wanted to woggle and Billy wanted to go to Spain.

Billy told Mr Bennet, and Mr Bennet said, '*Choose!*'

Owl and Billy and Woggly Man talked it over, and they decided.

'We choose going to Spain,' said Billy.

'Spain is a long way to walk,' said Mr Bennet. 'Further than the park. I don't know that my legs would take me.'

'You could go on my trike,' said Billy.

'Right across the sea and through France, down to Spain?' said Mr Bennet.

'On your motorbike then,' said Billy.

'I don't think we'd all fit,' said Mr Bennet. 'Better stick to the tricycle.'

'You won't fit on the tricycle,' Billy pointed out.

'But you will,' said Mr Bennet. 'You three

go on the tricycle, and I'll stay here.'

So Owl and Billy and Woggly Man got on the tricycle.

'Which way do I go?' Billy asked.

'Twenty times round the back yard, and then stop at the airport,' said Mr Bennet.

'Where's the airport?' said Billy.

'In the kitchen,' said Mr Bennet.

So Billy and Owl and the Woggly Man went whizz-whizz-whizzing eighteen-nineteen-twenty times round the back yard, and then they stopped and got off the tricycle, and came into the kitchen.

'Buenos dias, Señores!' said Mr Bennet, but Owl didn't know what that meant, until Mr Bennet told him it meant 'Hullo, sirs!' in Spanish, and then Mr Bennet put them on the plane. The plane was two kitchen chairs with a brush laid across for the wings. They got into their seats and Mr Bennet said, 'Los billetes, Señor?' and Owl didn't know what he meant but Mr Bennet told Billy that 'billete' was the Spanish word for ticket, and Billy showed him their tickets.

'Gracias, Señores,' said Mr Bennet. (That means 'Thank you, sirs,' in Spanish.) Then the plane took off and flew all the way to Madrid (which is in Spain), where they were just in time for Spanish tea. Mr Bennet gave Billy el plátano, which was a banana, and el caramelo, which was a toffee, and Billy said 'Gracias' each time, because he was in

Spain. Owl and Woggly Man didn't say it, because they didn't speak Spanish.

Then Billy's mum came.

'Ah! La Señora!' cried Mr Bennet, and he got Billy's mum to show them how to do a Spanish Dance. Then Billy did one too, but Owl and Woggly Man didn't, because they were no good at dancing.

Then Billy's mum said, 'Back to the hacienda!' and they all had to go home, but first they flew back to the airport and then Billy had to trike ride to Mr Bennet's and *then* they went home.

'Hasta la vista! called Mr Bennet, as they went down the road.

'That means "Cheerio till the next time"' said Billy's mum.

'When is the next time?' asked Billy.

'Tomorrow!' said Mum.

Billy thought about it, and then he spoke to Owl, and then he said, 'Yesterday was Moonday, and today is Chooseday *and* Twoes-day, so what day is tomorrow?'

'I don't know,' said Mum.

'I'll go back and ask Mr Bennet,' said Billy.

'Oh no you won't,' said Mum. 'You'll have to wait and see!'

3 Weddingsday

The next day was Dad's day off so he lay in bed for ages and read his paper, and then he got up and bumped around the house in his old clothes, and then Mum said, 'Time you did the garden!'

'Right!' said Dad, and he had a cup of tea, and then he went out and watered the strawberries, and then he sat down in the deckchair and went to sleep.

'I don't call that doing the garden!' Mum said, looking out of the window.

'Neither do I! said Billy.

'Revenge!' said Mum.

And she got the watering can, and watered Dad!

'Augh!' gasped Dad, as the water sprayed all over him.

'Got you!' said Mum.

Then Dad got the watering can, and he watered Mum.

'What about me?' said Billy.

And they both watered Billy.

'Now we'll all grow like weeds!' said Dad.

Billy watered Owl, because he wanted Owl to grow too.

'Oh Billy!' wailed Mum. 'Poor Owl! He's soaked!' and she pegged Owl up on the line to dry.

'I don't think Owl likes being pegged, Mum,' said Billy, looking at Owl up on the line.

'I'm not sure he liked being watered, Billy,' said Mum. 'Owls don't dry out as quickly as little boys.'

'Is that because Owls are made of pillow-cases, Mum?' said Billy.

'Probably,' said Mum.

'I hope he'll dry out in time for going to Mr Bennet's,' said Billy anxiously.

'I'm not sure you ought to go to Mr Bennet's today, Billy,' said Mum. 'He's a

very old man, and you've been round to play with him a lot. I think he needs another Moonday.'

'With Moon games?' said Billy, hopefully.

'No Moon Games, Billy,' said Mum. 'Just *moon*ing.'

'What's all this about?' said Dad.

So Billy told him about Monday that was Moonday, and Tuesday that was Twoesday and Chooseday.

'And today is Wednesday, but I don't know what Space day it will be,' said Billy. 'That's why I've got to go to Mr Bennet's to find out. This is my holiday, and Mr Bennet said that every day of my holiday was a special day!'

'I think *I* know,' said Dad, suddenly.

'No you don't,' said Billy. He knew Dad didn't, because Dad wasn't a Spaceman, and the Space Days were a Space Secret between Billy and Mum and Owl and Woggly Man, nobody else.

'I do because I'm a very *cunning* dad,' said Dad.

'What day is it then?' demanded Billy.

'It's Weedingsday!' said Dad.

'What do people do on Weedingsday?' asked Billy.

'Weed!' said Dad. 'Weed the garden!' And he got Billy a trowel and a basin and showed Billy the weeds. Billy weeded them.

For ages and ages and ages.

'I've almost run out of weeds, Dad,' Billy said, but Dad didn't say anything. He just lay in the deckchair with his newspaper over his face.

Then Billy saw some big weeds.
They were in the greenhouse.
Billy weeded them.

Billy's dad was cross!

'My tomatoes!' Dad shouted. 'All my lovely tomato plants!' And he rushed up the garden to the greenhouse with Billy's basin, to see if he could replant them.

'What's Dad planting weeds for?' Billy asked Mum.

'Must be for next Weedingsday,' said Mum. 'So you'll have something to weed.' But she told Billy to keep out of Dad's way, just for a while.

'I'll go to Mr Bennet's,' said Billy.

'That might not be such a bad idea,' said Mum, and she unpegged Owl from the line and Billy and Owl went off to Mr Bennet's.

'Good morning, Mr Bennet,' said Billy.

'Good morning,' said Mr Bennet. He was out in his front garden zoom-varooming his motorbike.

'Owl says you should be weeding,' said Billy.

'Why?' said Mr Bennet.

'Because it is Weedingsday!' said Billy, and he told Mr Bennet all about the weeding in the garden, and the extra special big weeds in Dad's greenhouse.

'My dad got very cross,' said Billy. 'But I don't know what about.'

'I think he was cross because he got the day *wrong*, Billy,' said Mr Bennet. 'That's enough to make anyone cross.'

Billy told Owl, and Owl said that Mr Bennet was probably right. Then owl wanted to know what day it really was, and Billy asked Mr Bennet.

Mr Bennet went: which means 'I'll have to think about it'.

'Don't you know?' said Billy.

'I know, but I've forgotten,' said Mr Bennet. 'What day do you think it *might* be?'

Billy asked Owl, and Owl said it might be Owl's day, so Billy told Mr Bennet.

'No, it can't be Owl's day because Space Days sound like earth days, Billy,' said Mr Bennet. '*Moon*day sounds like *Mon*day.'

'And Chooseday sounds like Tuesday!' said Billy.

'What day sounds like Wednesday?' asked Mr Bennet.

'Weedingsday!' said Billy. 'Dad was right, and you were wrong, Mr Bennet. It must be

Weedingsday, because Weedingsday sounds like Wednesday.'

'No it isn't,' said Mr Bennet. 'I got a Space Message about it just before you came, Billy, and the Space Message said: IT ISN'T WEEDINGSDAY: IT'S WEDDINGSDAY.'

'What's Weddingsday?' asked Billy.

'Somebody's getting married!' said Mr Bennet.

'Is it me?' said Billy.

'No,' said Mr Bennet. 'Getting married is for grown-ups.'

Billy told Owl, and Owl said that Mr Bennet had probably got it wrong, just like silly Dad.

'Owl thinks grown-ups getting married isn't much fun,' said Billy. 'He thinks you must have got it wrong.'

'It *might* be fun,' said Mr Bennet.

'How might it be fun?' said Billy.

'It depends who is getting married,' said Mr Bennet. 'If it's someone we know, then we throw things at them and tie things on their cars and shout and cheering and get our photographs taken – So we'd better go

and find out who is getting married,' said
Mr Bennet.

'Where do we go?' said Billy.

'To the wedding!' said Mr Bennet.

He put on his jacket and Owl and Billy
and Mr Bennet got an old boot and some
string out of Mr Bennet's spare room and
they all went down the road to the shop and
Mr Bennet bought a bag of something.

'What's that?' said Billy.

'Confetti!' said Mr Bennet. 'Little bits of
coloured paper!'

'What for?' said Billy.

'For throwing all over the someone who is
getting married if it is someone we know!'
said Mr Bennet. 'If it isn't someone we
know, we take it back home again.'

They went down the Main Street, but
they didn't see anybody getting married.
And there wasn't anybody getting married
at the park, either.

Then Mr Bennet saw the car. It was
outside a big hotel, and lots of people were
running round it tying things onto the back,
and squirting it with soap suds.

'That's it!' said Mr Bennet. 'There, where

the Getting Married is going on!'

'The people who are getting married will be very cross when they see their car,' said Billy.

'I don't think they will,' said Mr Bennet, and he took out his string and tied the old boot onto the back of the car, beside lots of other old boots and tin cans and saucepans. 'It's just to make the car look pretty,' he told Billy.

Billy hadn't anything to make the car look pretty with except Owl, so he put Owl in Mr Bennet's boot, but he didn't tell Mr Bennet because Mr Bennet was busy talking to some ladies in big hats who had come out of the hotel.

Then the hotel doors opened.

Miss Murphy came out of the hotel, with Mr Monk. Miss Murphy was Billy's teacher, and Mr Monk was P3's teacher, but they didn't look like teachers. They were all dressed up.

All the ladies in big hats charged! They started throwing confetti at the two teachers!

'Can I throw some?' Billy said.

'Yes,' said Mr Bennet.

39

And Billy went right up to Miss Murphy and threw his confetti over her.

'Hullo, Billy dear!' said Miss Murphy. And she kissed Billy.

'Atta boy, Billy!' said Mr Monk.

'Are you marrying Miss Murphy?' Billy asked him, because he was worried about wasting his confetti if it was someone else.

'Yes!' said Mr Monk, happily.

'Why?' said Billy.

'Because I love her!' said Mr Monk, and all the ladies cheered and Billy got his photograph taken and everybody shouted and danced about and then Miss Murphy and Mr Monk got into the car which was covered in things and the car drove away.

'What's the matter, Billy?' said Mr Bennet. 'You got your photo taken and you threw your confetti and . . . where's Owl?'

And Billy told him.

'Oh dear!' said Mr Bennet.

'I thought Owl would make the car look pretty,' said Billy. 'I didn't know they were going to drive it!'

'Well, I'm afraid Owl's gone now, Billy,' said Mr Bennet.

'Don't worry,' said Billy. 'Miss Murphy
knows Owl. She'll bring him back.

'I *hope* she will, Billy,' said Mr Bennet.

'Miss Murphy always brings Owl back
when I leave him places,' said Billy.

'But maybe not on her wedding day,' said

Mr Bennet.

'Why not?'

'Because she'll have lots and lots of things to do and people to talk to, Billy,' said Mr. Bennet. 'She'll be rushing about all over the place, and she might not notice Owl.'

'Oh,' said Billy.

'Let's just hope she will,' said Mr Bennet.

And they both went sadly home.

'Owl's gone on honeymoon!' Mr Bennet told Mum, and Mum took Billy on her knee and said how sorry she was.

'Miss Murphy will bring Owl back!' said Billy.

'Maybe she *won't*, this time, Billy,' said Mum. 'Miss Murphy will be very busy and she might not notice Owl. She might just throw Mr Bennet's old boot away when they clean the car, without looking to see if Owl is inside it.'

'She *will* notice!' said Billy. 'I know, because she's my teacher!'

Then he went upstairs to his room and told Woggly Man about it, and they sat at the window and watched for Owl to come and then . . .

Purrrrrr.

A big taxi came down Billy's street, and stopped outside Billy's door.

'It's Miss Murphy!' Billy shouted.

But it wasn't.

It was Miss Redmond, the headmistress at Billy's school.

Miss Redmond rang the doorbell, and Mum and Billy and Woggly Man answered the door.

'Good afternoon,' Miss Redmond said. 'I believe this boot belongs to Billy.'

And she handed Billy the boot, with Owl inside it.

Billy took Owl out and then he gave the boot back to Miss Redmond.

'Owl belongs to me, but the boot doesn't!' Billy said. 'The boot belongs to Mr Bennet.'

'Oh dear!' said Miss Redmond. 'Miss Murphy said you were to have it specially, Billy, because she's sent you a surprise inside it!'

And there was. In the boot, tied up in a pretty box, was a piece of white wedding cake from Miss Murphy's wedding.

Owl and Billy and Woggly Man had it for their tea.

'Did you enjoy Weddingsday, Billy?' asked Mum, when she was putting him to bed.

'Bits of it,' said Billy, and he told her

about the confetti and getting his photograph taken.

'And the cake,' said Mum. 'And getting
Owl back.'

'Y-e-s,' said Billy.

'And Miss Murphy getting married,' said
Billy's mum.

'Y-e-s,' said Billy. 'But Owl says Miss
Murphy might not come back and teach me
any more, now she's got married.'

'Tell Owl he's silly!' said Mum.

And Billy went to sleep remembering all
the nice things about Weddingsday, and
wondering what the next Space day would be.

4 Fairsday

'Mum,' said Billy the next morning, when they were out at the shops, 'What day is it today?'

'Thursday,' said Mum.

'What *Space* Day?' asked Billy.

'No idea, Billy,' said Mum.

'Space days *sound* like ordinary days,' Billy said. 'So it must be a day that sounds like Thursday.'

'GRRRSday!' said Mum, quickly, and she gave a dreadful grrr like a lion.

It made Owl jump.

'You scared Owl!' Billy said. 'Do it again!'

'GRRRR!' went Mum, and she scared the postman, who was going past on his bicycle.

He almost fell off.

'That was a *big* GRRRRR!' Billy said.

'You do one,' said Mum, and Billy went GRRRRRRRR!

Owl said it waas a better GRRRR than Mum's, but Billy didn't tell her.

When Billy got home he did his GRRRRR for Woggly Man, and he GRRRRR-ed through the window at Mrs Wilkins and then he wanted to go and GRRRRR at the

Wilkins' baby, but Mum said he wasn't to because the Wilkins' baby might be scared.

'Like Owl,' said Billy.

'Owl's not a baby,' said Mum. 'Owl wouldn't cry, and be frightened. Wilkins' baby might. You wouldn't want to scare a little baby, would you?'

Billy thought about it. He didn't like the Wilkins' baby much, because it was a boring baby. It couldn't even crawl properly. But he didn't want to frighten it either.

'I don't think it is GRRRRsday anyway, Billy,' said Mum. 'I don't think I would like GRRRRsday, anymore than the Wilkins' baby would. I think it is probably PURRS-day!'

Billy thought about it, and then he asked Owl, and Owl said it might be.

'Do one!' Billy said to Mum. 'Do a purr!'

'I'm not very good at purrs, Billy,' Mum said, but she tried it just the same.

'PURRRRRR!' went Mum.

'GRRRRRing's more fun!' said Billy, and he went off with Owl to practise his GRRRRR so that it would be a better GRRRRR than Mum's.

GRRRRRRR! Billy went to the gate-post and

GRRRRRRRRR! Billy went to Henny's wheelchair, which was outside Henny's house without Henny in it
and

GRRRRRRRRRRRRRR! Billy went to Mr Bennet, at his house.

'What are you GRRRRRing for, Billy?' Mr Bennet said.

'I'm GRRRRRing because it is

GRRRRRsday!' said Billy.

And Mr Bennet went

'Is it PURRSday?' Billy said.

Mr Bennett went

'What day is it?' asked Billy, impatiently.

 went Mr Bennet.

'Forgotten again?' said Billy.

 went Mr Bennet.

'What about a Space Message?' said Billy, hopefully. 'Owl thinks you should get a Space Message about it.'

'I think Owl is right,' said Mr Bennet.

And he sat and thought and thought for a long time in his deckchair.

'How about FURSday?' he said, at last.

'Was that a Space Message?' Billy asked. Fursday didn't sound much fun. It would just be stroking cats and Billy didn't like cats much. Neither did Woggly Man, because Wilkins' cat often sat on him when he was out in the garden.

 went Mr Bennet.

'Wait for the message then,' said Billy.

'I think the Messages are *stuck*, Billy,' said Mr Bennet.

'Space Messages are never stuck,' said Billy.

'This one is,' said Mr Bennet. 'I haven't a clue what day it is. If it isn't GRRRRRsday or PURRsday or FURSday . . . how about HERSday?'

'What do you do on Hersday?' said Billy.

'You do what your mother tells you to, Billy,' said Mum, walking up behind him. 'And that means coming home for your lunch.'

'Will you be able to unstick the message without me?' Billy asked anxiously.

'I'll try,' said Mr Bennet.

'Try very hard,' said Mum.

Billy was just finishing his lunch when Mr Bennet came rushing in. 'I've unstuck the message, Billy!' he said. 'It's a Special Surprise, and we've got to hurry.'

'Can Owl come too?' asked Billy.

'Owl can come,' said Mr Bennet. 'But Woggly Man had better stay at home this time, because we might have our arms full coming back!'

'Back from where?' asked Mum.

'That's a secret!' said Mr Bennet, and he went off with Owl and Billy. They had to go down the street and then they had to go on the bus and then they had to get off the bus and get on *another* bus.

Billy sat upstairs in the second bus, and they got the front seat. Billy drove all the way to the Common, and he TOOTED and PEEPED just like the bus driver down below, and Billy didn't run over anyone.

'Owl wants us to go faster!' Billy told Mr Bennet.

'We can't go any faster than the bus,' said Mr Bennet.

Then they got off the bus and . . .

'I know what day it is!' shouted Billy. 'It's FAIRSDAY!

And it was!

Billy and Owl and Mr Bennet went on the dodgems, and Billy drove, and Mr Bennet got *bumped*.

Then they went on the helter-skelter. Mr Bennet sat down first and Billy sat on Mr Bennet and Owl sat on Billy and Mr Bennet got *banged*, landing on the mat.

They went on a roundabout, and Mr Bennet got *dizzy*, but Billy didn't.

Then Mr Bennet sat down, and Owl and Billy went on the rocket shoot and the

roundabout and the flying horses and the dodgems again, twice (Billy drove and Owl got bumped) and then the swings and then the *giant* slide and then the bouncy castle.

'You come on too,' Billy said to Mr Bennet, and Mr Bennet said, 'I've been bumped and banged and I'm not going to be bounced!'

He didn't go on.

But Billy did, three times.

Owl only went on the first time. He didn't go the second time and the third time because he had been bumped *and* banged *and* bounced, and he wanted to keep Mr Bennet company.

They got ice-creams, and balloons and 'I've been to the Fair' hats and a squeaker and they went home on the bus, and Billy squeaked all the way and then he ran into his own house and he SQUEEEAKED so loudly that Mum almost dropped her cup of tea.

She GRRRRed at Billy.

And Billy SQUEEEEAKED back:

SQUEEAK! SQUEEEAK! SQUEEEAK!

'That's enough, Billy!' said Mum.

SQUEEEAK! went Billy, one last time,
and then he stopped.

'Where's Mr Bennet?' said Mum.

'Gone home!' said Billy, and he told Mum
all about Mr Bennet being bumped and
banged and not bounced and about driving
the bus and going on the helter-skelter and

the roundabout and the flying horses and the dodgems (three times) and the swings and the giant slide and the bouncy castle, and he showed her his 'I've been to the Fair' hat and his squeaker, but he couldn't show her his ice-cream, because the bit that hadn't melted was inside him, and the bit that had was all over his T-shirt.

'It was a chocky one, Mum,' Billy said.

'I can *see* that, Billy,' said Mum, looking at Owl, who had got a bit chocky-looking himself. 'You know what I think? I think we both ought to go straight round to Mr Bennet's and thank him very much for giving you such a lovely Fairsday.'

And they did.

They rang Mr Bennet's door, but he didn't answer.

He didn't answer, because he was fast asleep in his big chair, in his 'I've been to the Fair' hat.

They could see him through the window, but Mum said not to bang it and wake him up.

'Must be Snoozeday now, Billy!' she said.

And Owl said it must be Snoresday.

They were both right, even though it
didn't sound like Thursday at all!

5 *Pieday*

The next morning Mum wouldn't let Billy go round to Mr Bennet's.

'Mr Bennet played with you on Monday and Tuesday and Wednesday and Thursday, Billy,' said Mum. 'I expect he needs a bit of a rest.'

'He had a rest yesterday,' said Billy, remembering Snoresday.

'He's not as young as he used to be, Billy.'

'Then I'll never know what Space Day it is!' said Billy.

'Yes you will,' said Mum, firmly. 'I think I know. It is Myday! And on Myday we have a nice quiet day at home, and don't bother Mr Bennet.'

'What do we have a nice quiet day *doing*?' asked Billy.

'You can help me with the dishes for a start!' Mum said.

'Owl doesn't want to help with the dishes,' Billy said.

'Nobody asked Owl,' said Mum. 'I'm asking you.'

Billy helped with the dishes, but it went a bit wrong, because Billy decided to show Owl how to blow bubbles with soap suds.

Billy's bubbles floated all over the kitchen, and they popped and popped and popped, popping soap suds over everything.

Mum had to clean all the soap suds up.

Billy and Owl and Woggly Man went out to the garden while she was doing it, to have a nice quiet football match.

C-R-A-S-H! went the cucumber frame.

'Billy!' Mum shouted.

'It was Owl,' Billy said, but Mum didn't believe him.

She didn't believe him about the broken roses either, although Billy told her it was the ball that broke the roses.

'They were goalposts, Mum,' he said. 'We had to have goalposts.'

'Oh, go into the house and keep out of my way, Billy,' said Mum. 'Play something *quietly*.'

So Owl and Billy played throwing Woggly Man down the stairs, *quietly*.

It was a great game. They threw Woggly Man right from the top of the stairs, with Billy's handkerchief tied on for a parachute.

The fourth time Billy missed.

S-M-A-S-H!

'Oh Billy!' said Mum, looking at the smashed flower bowl, with Woggly Man in the middle of it, and the water dripping all over the table.

'That was Woggly Man, Mum,' said Billy. 'He didn't fly straight.'

While Mum was clearing up, Billy gave Owl a nice quiet bath.

Things got *quietly* wet.

Then Billy cleaned the water up with the brush. It was the yard brush, and it made the carpet sort of streaky, because Billy had used it on the garden to flatten out the football pitch.

'Oh *no!*' wailed Mum, when she saw the carpet. 'This just isn't my day!'

'I didn't think it was,' said Billy.

'Go downstairs and sit and DON'T MOVE!' said Mum.

Billy went downstairs and sat and didn't move, but he thought.

When Mum came downstairs again, Billy said, 'I think it must be Cryday, Mum.'

'Cryday doesn't sound very nice, Billy,' said Mum. 'I haven't been as cross as all that, have I?'

'You were a bit,' said Billy, and Mum hugged him.

'It certainly *isn't* Cryday, Billy,' she said. 'But it can't be Myday either. It must be some other day. How exactly does this Space Message thing work?'

'Mr Bennet gets them,' said Billy. 'He sits down and closes his eyes and smokes his pipe for ages and ages and then he gets a message.'

'Let me try,' said Mum.

'You haven't got a pipe,' said Billy.

'I'll try without one,' said Mum.

And she sat and thought and thought and thought, and thought and thought and thought and . . .

'GOT IT!' she said. 'I was wrong. It isn't Myday!'

'What day is it then?' said Billy.

'A day that sounds just like Myday, but isn't,' said Mum. And she told Billy what day it really was.

'Can I do it?' Billy said.

'We'll do it together!' said Mum.

Then she took Billy into the kitchen and she got out a rolling pin and some flour and made some pastry and let Billy roll it. She got a dish and put the pastry in it and then she sent Billy out to the garden for apples. Mum got some sugar and she peeled the apples and she put in the sugar and some other things and popped the whole lot in the oven.

'When will it be ready, Mum?' Billy asked.

'Just in time for Mr Bennet's tea, Billy!' said Mum. 'Can I take it round to him?' Billy asked, and Mum said he could.

And so . . .

just at Mr Bennet's tea-time . . .

his doorbell went . . .

BRINNG! BRINNG! BRINNG!

And Mr Bennet opened the door.

'Hullo, Billy!', he said.

'Hullo, Mr Bennet,' said Billy. 'I bet you don't know what day it is.'

'Friday,' said Mr Bennet.

'It's not Friday,' said Billy. 'It's PIEDAY! and here it is!'

And he gave Mr Bennet the Great Ginormous Apple Pie they had made for his tea.

'Mum said to thank you very much for everything and here's your pie for Pieday!' said Billy, and then he added, looking at the pie, 'I don't think she would mind if you gave a bit to Owl.'

'And you?' said Mr Bennet.

'And me,' said Billy.

They had an Apple Pie Feast and Billy told Mr Bennet about Mum getting Myday wrong.

'She says you're not as young as you used to be,' said Billy.

'Is that so?' said Mr Bennet.

'Yes,' said Billy. 'You need to sleep a lot and you snore, like this!'

And he made a Mr Bennet snoring noise, left over from Snoresday.

'I don't!' said Mr Bennet.

'You do,' said Billy.

'Hmmph!' said Mr Bennet, but he wasn't really cross, because he gave Billy and Owl some more of his sweets before he sent them back to thank Mum very much for a lovely Pieday.

6 Sat-on-day

'It's Sat-on-day today, Billy,' said Mr Bennet, firmly. 'Sat-on-day is the day I sit in my chair all day, because I've got to save my strength for Funday.'

'Is Funday tomorrow?' said Billy.

'Yes,' said Mr Bennet.

Billy told Owl and Owl said that Funday sounded great but he wasn't so sure about Sat-on-day, and Sat-on-day was the day it *was*.

'You can have a different day if you want to,' said Mr Bennet. 'But I'm not having it with you. You have my Space permission to think up your own day, instead of Sat-on-day.'

Billy took Owl home to think about it. They thought about it in the garden. They had to think of days that sounded like Saturday but weren't, which is the way you think of Space Days.

First Billy thought it might be Batterday. So he went and battered the bins until Mum stopped him.

Then Owl thought of Clatterday, and they clattered the bins they'd been battering, because Mum had told them to stop battering, but she hadn't told them to stop clattering.

'Billy!' Mum shouted. 'Stop that at once!'

'It's Clatterday!' Billy shouted back, but Mum said he had to stop it just the same.

Then Billy thought of *another* day.

It was Fatterday.

Billy stuffed one of Mum's cushions in his jersey and he went round the house being fat like Miss Henshawe, but Mum said that wasn't very nice because Miss Henshawe couldn't help being fat, she was just built that way.

'Not like you, Mum,' said Billy, and Mum laughed and said it was Flatterday, was it?

'What's Flatterday, Mum?' Billy asked.

'A day when you go round saying nice things about people and flattering them,' said Mum.

So Billy went up to Woggly Man and said, 'What a nice Woggly Man you are!' and then he *flattered* him all over the carpet.

'What are you doing to Woggly Man, Billy?' Mum asked. 'You'll break him.'

'I'm World Boxing Championing and I'm flattering him, like you said,' said Billy. 'He was standing up, but now he's flattered, because I flattered him!'

Mum told Billy that flattering didn't mean flattening people out, it meant saying things about how wonderful they were, whether you believed the things or not.

'That's silly,' said Billy.

'I agree,' said Mum.

'I don't like Flatterday,' said Billy.

'What about Hatterday, then?' said Mum, and she got her rain hat and put it on Billy.

'Owl hasn't got a hat,' said Billy.

'I don't think Owls wear hats, Billy,' said Mum.

Billy asked Owl and Owl said that that was right, but what about Woggly Man?'

'I don't know about Woggly Man,' said Mum. 'I haven't got a hat for him.'

Billy found one. It was a flowerpot.

Then Mum said, 'Let's stop having Space Days, and have something to eat instead.'

And they did.

When they had finished Billy said, 'What day will it be now, Mum?'

'I don't know, Billy,' said Mum.

But Dad did.

He said it was 'Owzaterday!' and he got some stumps and Billy's bat and ball and they all played cricket in the back garden. Billy was the bowler and Dad was the batsman and Woggly Man was wicket keeper and Owl was Owl, because Owls don't play cricket. Every time Dad missed the ball Billy shouted '*Owzat!*'

It was a long, long game, and everybody was tired out when it was finished, so they sat on the rug in the garden and had Natterday.

'Natterday is when you talk a lot,' said Dad, and Billy nattered and nattered and nattered.

'Now we're having What's-the-matter-day!' said Dad. 'Whats-the-matter-with-you that makes you keep having funny days?'

It's Mr Bennet's fault,' said Billy. 'He said I was to think of my own Space Days.'

'Why don't you go and tell him about all the days you've had then, Billy?' said Dad.

And Billy did.

He woke Mr Bennet up in the garden and he told him about Batterday and Clatterday and Fatterday – which didn't mean flattening people – and Hatterday and Owzaterday and Natterday and What's-the-Matter-day.

'They all *must* be Space Days, because they sound like Saturday,' said Billy.

'The real Space Day is Sat-on-day!' said Mr Bennet. 'I know, because I've been having it, all day!'

'Did you enjoy it?' Billy asked.

'Yes!' said Mr Bennet.

'Then it must be right!' said Billy, and Owl said he thought so too.

7 *Funday*

The next day was Sunday, the very last day of Billy's holidays before he went back to school.

'It's Funday!' he told Mum. 'Mr Bennet says so.'

Mum thought about it. Then she said, 'Fun for who?'

'For me and Owl and Woggly Man and Mr Bennet,' said Billy. 'Mr Bennet sat in his chair all day yesterday and he said we'd have Funday today to make up for it!'

'I suppose he knows what he's doing!' Mum said, but she wouldn't let Billy go round to Mr Bennet's until after lunchtime.

'Hullo, Mr Bennet,' Billy said, when Mr

Bennet opened the door. 'Today's Funday!'

 went Mr Bennet.

'Owl wants to know what we're doing on Funday, Mr Bennet?' Billy said.

And Mr Bennet went

'I thought you'd have already thought about it!' said Billy. 'You had all Sat-on-day to think about it, sitting on your bottom.'

 went Mr Bennet.

'What were you doing on Sat-on-day then?' Billy demanded.

'Sitting on my bottom,' said Mr Bennet. 'That's what Sat-on-days are for.'

'We want to know about Fundays!' said Billy.

And Mr Bennet went again.

'All right!' said Billy. '*Do* it!'

And Mr Bennet sat down and thought

and thought and thought for a long, long
time and then he said, 'Hold on, I'm getting
a message!'

Owl told Billy to stop Mr Bennet getting a
message, in case the message said it wasn't
Funday after all, and Mr Bennet had got the
days mixed up again.

Billy told Mr Bennet, and Mr Bennet

said, 'It's not that sort of message. It's a what sort of Funday is it sort of message and the message says: S A U S A G E S!'

'Sausages?' said Billy, and he told Owl.

'Owl thinks that that's a funny message, Mr Bennet,' said Billy.

'There's another bit coming, Billy,' said Mr Bennet, puffing slowly on his pipe. 'It says: T I D D L E R S!'

'Does that mean little sausages?' said Billy.

 went Mr Bennet.

And then he got more of the message.
The next bit said: TENT.

'Sausages, tiddlers and tent?' said Mr Bennet. 'What does that mean? Do you know?'

And Billy went (which means no) because he didn't.

'Hold on!' said Mr Bennet. 'Two more bits are coming. One says, BACK FIELD and the other says RIVER.'

'What does that mean?' said Billy.

'Haven't a clue!' said Mr Bennet. 'We'd better ask your mum.'

So they went down to Billy's house.

'We've got a Space Message and we don't know what it means,' Mr Bennet told her.

'It was Sausages-Tiddlers-Tent-Back Field and River, Mum,' said Billy.

'We thought you might know what it means,' said Mr Bennet.

'I think I *do*!' said Mum.

And she sent Billy rushing up the stairs to get Dad's tent from the spare room. Then she got some sausages from the fridge, and Billy's pond net from Billy's room and she put her jeans on and then she said, 'Off we go!'

'Where to?' said Billy.

'The back field, by the river!' said Mum.

And off they all went.

When they got to the river, Billy and Mr Bennet put up Dad's tent and then Billy and Mr Bennet went into the wood and they brought some old sticks and Mr Bennet made a fireplace and Mum said, 'Right! Now we cook the sausages!'

'What in?' said Billy.

'The frying pan,' said Mum.

But they hadn't brought the frying pan with them, because Mr Bennet's message didn't say anything about frying pans. It said: Sausages-Tiddlers-Tent-Back Field and River.

'Your message was wrong, Mr Bennet!' said Billy.

'Oh no it wasn't, Billy,' said Mr Bennet, and he got two forks from Dad's tent pack and he showed Billy how to cook sausages without a pan.

Mr Bennet got very hot in the face, and Billy got very smoky and Mum burnt her finger, but the sausages were brilliant.

'Now! Tiddlers!' said Mr Bennet.

And Billy and Mr Bennet fished for tiddlers in the river.

Owl and Mum and Woggly Man watched, because Owls and Mums and Woggly Men aren't very good at catching tiddlers.

Billy and Mr Bennet went SPLASH!

And SPLOSH!

But they didn't catch a single tiddler.

'I don't think you're doing that the right way!' Mum said, and she rolled up her jeans and went into the river with Billy, and Mr Bennet went to talk to Owl and Woggly Man and smoke his pipe.

Mum crept up on the tiddlers, like this:

And then when they swam into the net she went like this:

And she caught . . .
LOTS!

'Brilliant!' said Billy. 'Catch some more!'
Mum caught some more. Then she
showed Billy how to do it and Billy caught
some and then Mum wanted another go and
she stepped on a big stone and
S P L O O O S H !

'Ooaah!' wailed Mum. 'Help!'
Billy saved her.
'What happened?' Mr Bennet said, wak-
ing up.

88

'The tiddlers caught *me*!' said Mum.

Then Billy took Woggly Man for a paddle while Mum dried out and then Mum and Billy put the tiddlers back into the water so that they could grow up to be fish. Billy helped Mr Bennet to clear up the fire with water and stones, so that the wind wouldn't light the flames after they'd gone and set all the bushes on fire. Then they packed up Dad's tent and started home.

Owl and Billy and Woggly Man talked all the way home, *natter-natter-natter*!

And Mr Bennet smoked his pipe all the way home, *puff-puff-puff*.

And Mum went *squealch-squealch-squealch* all the way home, because she was still wet.

She squealched right into the kitchen, and she squealched Dad when he laughed at her.

'I can see that you all enjoyed yourselves!' said Dad, and Billy said, 'It was the best Funday ever!'

'And the day after Funday is Schoolday!' said Mum. 'No more Space Days until you get your next holidays!'

Billy thought about it. 'Space Days are more fun than Schooldays, Mum,' he said. 'I

wish there could be Space Days always.'

'Tell that to Mr Bennet!' said Mum.

'I'd like to *be* Mr Bennet,' said Billy. 'Mr Bennet makes fun happen for other people, doesn't he? Like me and Owl and Woggly Man.'

'And me!' said Mum.

90

'He's a very special old man,' said Dad.

'He's a Spa . . .' Billy began, but then he stopped. Dad didn't know about Mr Bennet, and Billy wasn't going to tell him.

It was a Space Secret between Mr Bennet and Billy and Mum and Owl and Woggly Man, and Billy knew how to keep Space Secrets.

He went to bed with Owl and Woggly Man, and they talked and talked and talked together about the Space Days, until Mum tucked them up and put the light out, and then Billy went to sleep, and *dreamed* about Space Days instead!

Also available from Mammoth Paperbacks

Martin Waddell

Owl and Billy

It's a whole week until Billy can start school. Until
then, he's only got Owl to play with. Then a friendly
Spaceman moves into the street and before long Billy
has an exciting new friend.

Mary Hoffman

Specially Sarah

It's not always easy being the oldest in the family.
Sarah is the first to go to school, the first to make
new friends and the first to be invited to a birthday
party. And when she becomes an older sister for the
second time, there's even more excitement . . .

Margaret Greaves

Hetty Pegler, Half-Witch

Ben, Jane and Toby are none too pleased when their
mother invites a strange child to their house for a
holiday. But when they discover that this thin,
green-eyed girl is called Hetty Pegler and is a
half-witch they are thrilled. So it is hardly surprising
when her spells have unexpected and often hilarious
results! After all she is only half a witch!

Tony Bradman

Dilly – The Worst Day Ever

Dilly is the *naughtiest* dinosaur in the whole world and he has a 150 mph scream!

This is the fifth collection of Dilly adventures and Dilly is trying to turn over a new leaf. But everything goes wrong! The harder he tries, the worse things get . . .

Also available: DILLY THE DINOSAUR
DILLY'S MUDDY DAY
DILLY TELLS THE TRUTH
DILLY AND THE HORROR FILM

A selected list of titles available from Mammoth

While every effort is made to keep prices low, it is sometimes necessary to increase prices at short notice. Mammoth paperbacks reserve the right to show new retail prices on covers which may differ from those previously advertised in the text or elsewhere.

The prices shown below were correct at the time of going to press.

☐ 416 96490 7	Dilly the Dinosaur	*Tony Bradman*	£1.99
☐ 416 51910 5	The Witch's Big Toe	*Ralph Wright*	£1.75
☐ 416 95910 5	The Grannie Season	*Joan Phipson*	£1.75
☐ 416 58270 2	Listen To This Story	*Grace Hallworth*	£1.75
☐ 416 10382 0	The Knights of Hawthorn Crescent	*Jenny Koralek*	£1.50
☐ 416 13822 5	It's Abigail Again	*Moira Miller*	£1.99
☐ 416 11972 7	Lucy Jane at the Ballet	*Susan Hampshire*	£1.50
☐ 416 06432 9	Alf Gorilla	*Michael Grater*	£1.75
☐ 416 10362 6	Owl and Billy	*Martin Waddell*	£1.50
☐ 416 13122 0	Hetty Pegler, Half-Witch	*Margaret Greaves*	£1.75
☐ 416 57290 1	Flat Stanley	*Jeff Brown*	£1.50
☐ 416 00572 1	Princess Polly to the Rescue	*Mary Lister*	£1.50
☐ 416 00552 7	Non Stop Nonsense	*Margaret Mahy*	£1.75
☐ 416 10322 7	Claudius Bald Eagle	*Sam McBratney*	£1.75
☐ 416 03212 5	I Don't Want To!	*Bel Mooney*	£1.99

All these books are available at your bookshop or newsagent, or can be ordered direct from the publisher. Just tick the titles you want and fill in the form below.

Mammoth Paperbacks,   Cash Sales Department
P.O. Box 11, Falmouth,
Cornwall TR10 9EN

Please send cheque or postal order, no currency, for purchaser price quoted and allow the following for postage and packing;

UK   55p for the first book, 22p for the second book and 14p for each additional book ordered to a maximum charge of £1.75.

BFPO and Eire   55p for the first book, 22p for the second book and 14p for each next seven books, thereafter 8p per book.

Overseas   £1.00 for the first book plus 25p per copy for each additional
Customers   book.

NAME (Block letters) ....

ADDRESS ....

....